Thomas Nelson and Sons Ltd
Nelson House Mayfield Road
Walton-on-Thames Surrey
KT12 5PL UK

51 York Place
Edinburgh
EH1 3JD UK

Thomas Nelson (Hong Kong) Ltd
Toppan Building 10/F
22A Westlands Road
Quarry Bay Hong Kong

Thomas Nelson Australia
102 Dodds Street
South Melbourne
Victoria 3205
Australia

Nelson Canada
1120 Birchmount Road
Scarborough Ontario
M1K 5G4 Canada

Letterland was devised by Lyn Wendon and is part of
the *Pictogram* system © Lyn Wendon 1973-1986

ISBN 0-17-410162-7
NPN 9876

Printed in Italy

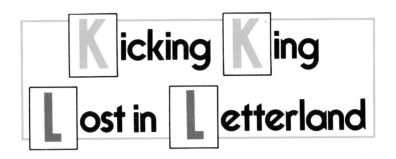

Kicking King Lost in Letterland

Written by
Lyn Wendon

Illustrated by
Jane Launchbury

Nelson

Letterland's king loves to play football. That is why everyone calls him the 'Kicking King'.

One day the Kicking King went into the Letterland sport shop to buy a new football. In the shop, he saw a strange boat hanging from the ceiling.

"What is that?" he asked, as he paid for his ball.
"That's a kayak," explained the shopkeeper. "The Eskimos use kayaks to paddle along the icy rivers of the far north."

"I'll buy the kayak, too," said the king. "If I learn to paddle a kayak, perhaps I can make my arms as strong as my legs."

Every day the king paddled his kayak around the biggest lake in Letterland. Soon his arms were so strong he could cross the lake in no time at all.

"I need a bigger lake," the king complained one morning to Dippy Duck, who was swimming nearby.

"Why don't you try the sea?" asked Dippy. "Shall I show you a quick way to get there?"

"Yes, please!" cried the king.
So off they went.

On the way, they passed the Lamp Lady's lighthouse, high up on a cliff above the sea. "Come and have some lunch with me," said Lucy, the Lamp Lady.

"Not now, thanks," said the Kicking King. He was too keen to try his kayak out on the sea to stop.

"Another time, then," called Lucy, as Dippy Duck led the way down to the sea.

The blue, sparkling water stretched away into the distance. "This will be much more exciting than paddling across the lake!" said the king.

Dippy Duck watched while the king pushed the kayak out to sea. He jumped in, waved goodbye and paddled off. Soon the king had gone beyond the lighthouse and vanished from sight.

"I hope he won't go too far," thought Dippy Duck. The sun was hot and she felt sleepy, so she decided to have a little snooze until the king came back.

It was so warm and comfortable on the beach that Dippy Duck's short snooze turned into a long sleep. When she woke up it was late afternoon. Where was the king?

"Perhaps he came back while I was asleep," she thought.
She waddled up to the lighthouse to ask Lucy, but she had not seen him.

Dippy Duck began to feel worried. "I expect he's having so much fun, he's forgotten what time it is," said Lucy "He will be back before dark."

The sun began to set, but there was still no sign of the Kicking King.

L ucy switched on the great lighthouse light. It shone its powerful beam far out to sea, but she could not see the kayak.

"I'm afraid the king must be lost," said the Lamp Lady. "We must launch the lifeboats to find him."

Five minutes later, lifeboats were dashing out in all directions looking for the Kicking King. An hour went by, but still the lifeboats did not find him.

It was not surprising that the lifeboats could not find the Kicking King. He was not at sea at all!

The king had enjoyed himself so much, that he paddled his kayak along the coast for many miles. He only turned around when the sun began to set.

As he headed back to the spot where he had left Dippy Duck, a strong current caught the boat. Crash! The kayak hit some rocks.

The Kicking King flew through the air and landed at the bottom of a cliff.

"Help! Help!" cried the king, but only the sea-gulls heard him. He looked at his kayak. It would never take him back now. Worse still, he could not find any way of walking up the cliff.

"I could kick myself," he said. "Now I am really stuck."

Soon the king saw the lifeboats looking for him out at sea.

"Why don't they look for me here?" he cried. "I would hate to spend the night on this cold beach. I must think of a way to tell them where I am – but how?"

*S*uddenly the king had an idea. "I know!" he said. "I'll turn my kayak into a kite!"

Soon he had made some bits of wood and canvas into the kite's body. Then he used some seaweed for its tail.

"All I need now is string," he thought. "But where can I find some?"

The Kicking King looked down at his feet. Then he took off his football boots and one sock…

As the sun set, the king ran along the beach with the kite. Woosh! Up it went, high above the rocks and right over the cliff. His plan was working, but was it too late? Would anyone see the kite?

Yes! Lucy, the Lamp Lady was out looking for the king. Imagine her surprise when she saw a strange-looking kite looming out of the darkness. It must be a signal from the king!

"I'm coming!" she called. With her long legs flying, she leapt down a secret path to the beach.

"Well done, Lucy. You found me!" cried the king.

"Yes," replied the Lamp Lady, "and now I can light your way home. Just follow me. Talk to me as we walk. Tell me what happened. We all thought we had lost our king!"

Lucy flashed a message to the lifeboats to let them know that the Kicking King was safe!

In no time at all, Kicking King and Lucy joined Dippy Duck back at the lighthouse. The lifeboat men came in, too.

"Perhaps you will have lunch with me now," said Lucy with a laugh.
"A very late lunch, that is! Or shall we all have a cup of tea?"

"Put on the kettle," cried the king.

Soon everyone was drinking tea and laughing about the day that the king got lost in Letterland.

THE END